cAptAiN
⭐WESOME
TO THE RESCUE!

By STAN KIRBY

Illustrated by
**GEORGE
O'CONNOR**

LITTLE SIMON
New York   London   Toronto   Sydney   New Delhi

 LITTLE SIMON

An imprint of Simon & Schuster Children's Publishing Division
1230 Avenue of the Americas, New York, New York 10020
Copyright © 2012 by Simon & Schuster, Inc. All rights reserved, including the right of reproduction in whole or in part in any form. LITTLE SIMON is a registered trademark of Simon & Schuster, Inc., and associated colophon is a trademark of Simon & Schuster, Inc. For information about special discounts for bulk purchases, please contact Simon & Schuster Special Sales at 1-866-506-1949 or business@simonandschuster.com. The Simon & Schuster Speakers Bureau can bring authors to your live event. For more information or to book an event contact the Simon & Schuster Speakers Bureau at 1-866-248-3049 or visit our website at www.simonspeakers.com.
Manufactured in the United States of America 0319 MTN
20 19 18 17 16 15
Library of Congress Cataloging-in-Publication Data
Kirby, Stan. Captain Awesome to the rescue! / by Stan Kirby ; illustrated by George O'Connor. — 1st ed. p. cm. Summary: When second-grader Eugene and his family move to a new neighborhood and he starts at a new school, he has a chance to bring out his superhero alter ego, Captain Awesome, to find the kidnapped class hamster. [1. Superheroes—Fiction. 2. Moving, Household—Fiction. 3. Schools—Fiction. 4. Hamsters—Fiction.] I. O'Connor, George, ill. II. Title. PZ7.K633529Cap 2012 [Fic]—dc23 2011014294
ISBN 978-1-4424-3561-2 (pbk)
ISBN 978-1-4424-4090-6 (hc)
ISBN 978-1-4424-3562-9 (eBook)

Table of Contents

CHAPTER 1

Here He Comes to Save the Day!

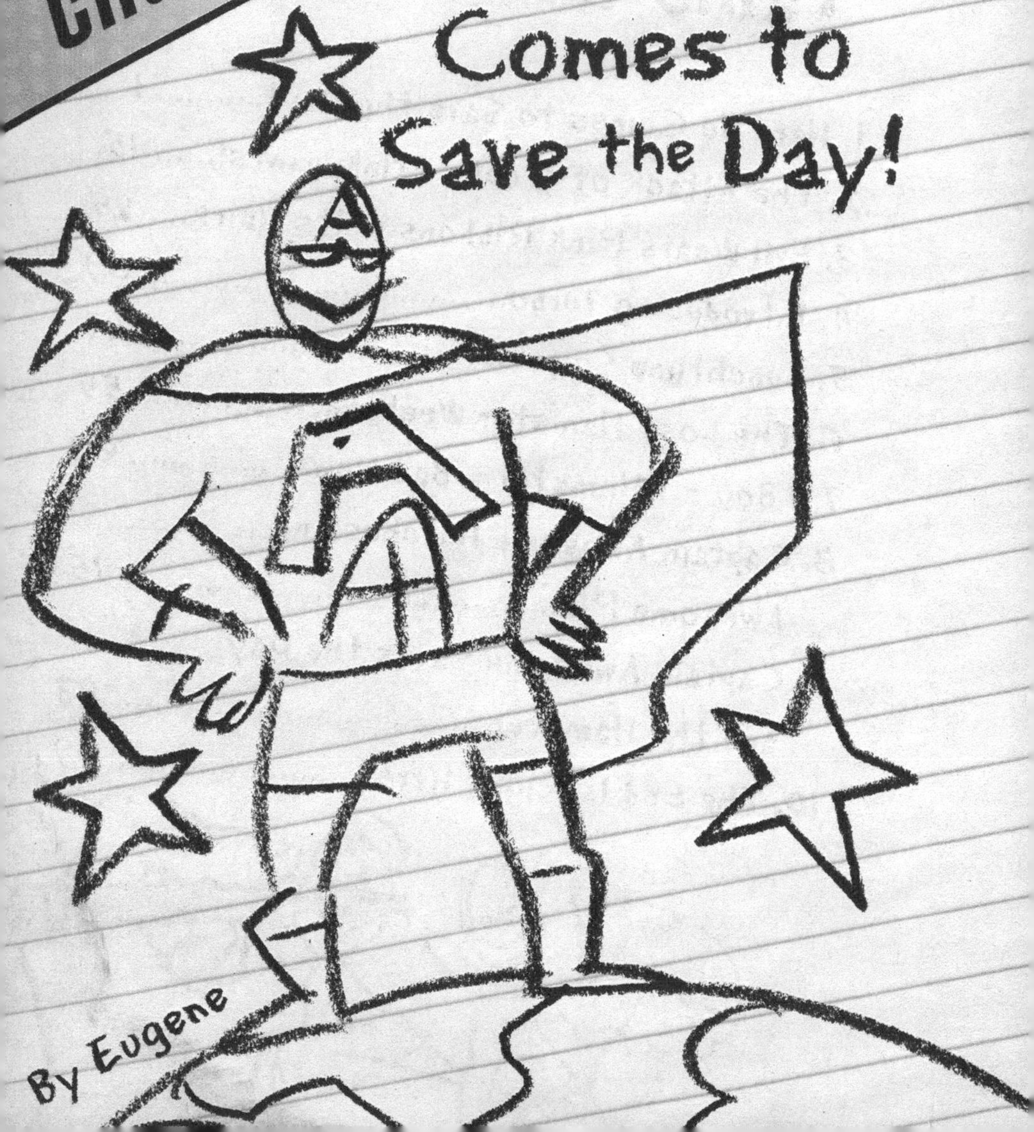

"**W**here's my Captain Awesome cape?" Eugene grumbled as he searched his closet. He tossed clothes back over his head, covering a stack of Super Dude comic books.

Psssst! Want to know a secret? It's the most hugest, gigantist, enormondoist secret ever. The boy looking for his cape is not just eight-year-old Eugene McGillicudy, son of Ned and Betsy, and brother to his little sister, Molly. He's also the superhero known as Captain Awesome!

Say it out loud:

CAPTAIN! AWESOME!

Eugene came up with that name himself. That's one of the cool things about being a superhero. You get to pick your own name. And if you're making up your own superhero name, it shouldn't be something lame like "Captain Just Okay." It should be mighty, like . . . Captain Awesome! MI-TEE!

Eugene plopped on the pile of clothes and crossed his arms. *Next time, I'll remember to follow Superhero Rule number one: Never let your mom pack your superhero*

stuff when you're moving to a new town. I bet Super Dude's mom never lost his cape.

Wait! You've never heard of Super Dude?! He's only THE coolest, bravest, heroist superhero of all time, and the one responsible for Eugene becoming Captain Awesome.

It all started the day Eugene's dad gave him his copy of Super Dude No. 1.

Sure, it might've looked like he was just giving Eugene the comic so he wouldn't tell his mother who ate the last of the chocolate-chocolate chip ice cream, but Eugene knew what his dad was secretly telling him: Since he's too busy with work and

dad-stuff like mowing lawns and telling Eugene to keep his elbows off the dinner table, and eating the last of his mom's chocolate-chocolate chip ice cream, it was up to Eugene to save the world from now on!

Eugene and his family had just moved to a new town for his dad's job called Sunnyview—he worked for Cherry Computers. ("Cherry's on Top!")

"Eugene!" his mom called from downstairs. "Can you please come down when you get a chance? I want to talk to you about school."

Oh, great! First she loses my cape and now she wants to talk about school! Eugene looked at the calendar on his wall. And tomorrow's my first day.

Hooray.

BY HOORAY I REALLY MEAN BARF! I DON'T

SUPER DUDE RETURNS

SCHOOL!

WANT TO GO TO A NEW SCHOOL!"

Eugene fell backward into his clothes pile and covered his head with his pajamas.

Things were really getting desperate! First his cape was missing, and now school talk?! Yuck! Could today get any worse?!

Eugene leaped to his feet and struck a superhero pose. "Miff ivnent da mime poo burry abut barf—" Eugene stopped and yanked the pajamas off his face. "This isn't the time to worry about BARF and new schools,"

Eugene said and punched his hand into his palm. "I need to find my cape or Captain Awesome won't be able to protect Sunnyview from the evil doings of bad guys like Queen Stinkypants, Baron Von Booger, or Dr. Spinach. Letting the bad guys win is

BAM!

worse than
homework ...
on a weekend!"

Evildoers all over Sunnyview had better beware, because Captain Awesome was going to ferret them out just like a, well, a ferret ferrets stuff, except he'll be wearing a superhero outfit and he won't have a furry tail.

Captain Awesome will give bad

guys his famous one-two punch
and tell them to change their ways
and become good guys . . . or . . .
he'll . . . tell their parents.

And if you think the Captain Awesome one-two punch sounds scary, you should see a super-villain's angry parents. Bad guys hate to lose, but they hate being grounded even more!

But instead of fighting evil this morning, Eugene was digging through all the boxes in his new bedroom looking for his superhero cape.

"I'll bet Super Dude never had days like this." Eugene sighed.

And that's when Eugene heard it! The evil "Goo!" and "Gaaah!"

of his archenemy . . . **Queen Stinkypants from Planet Baby!**

CHAPTER 2

The Attack of Queen Stinkypants!

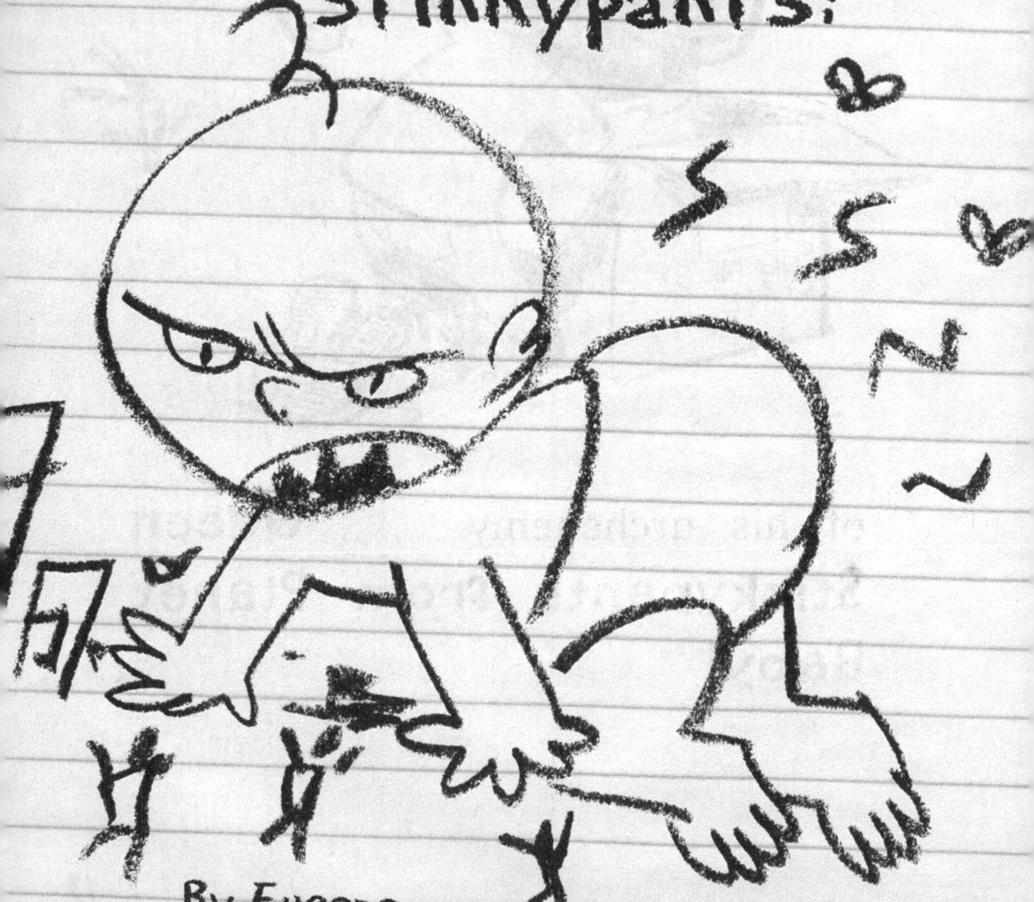

By Eugene

Left foot. Right foot. "Goo." Fall down. Get up. Left foot. Right foot. Fall down. "Gaah." Get up.

"I'd know those sounds any-where!" Eugene raced to his bed-room door and peeked down the hallway . . . and there she was! "QUEEN STINKYPANTS!" he cried. "My archenemy from Planet Baby!"

Even from the safety of his secret hideout,

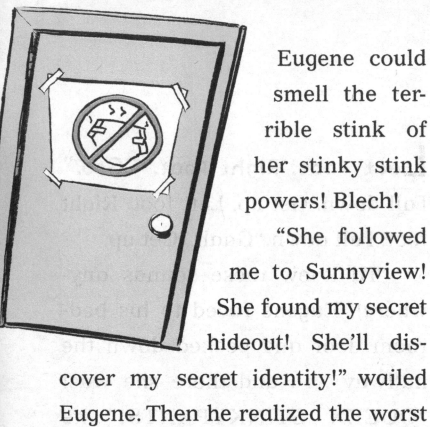

Eugene could smell the terrible stink of her stinky stink powers! Blech!

"She followed me to Sunnyview! She found my secret hideout! She'll discover my secret identity!" wailed Eugene. Then he realized the worst thing of all! "AHHHH! She'll drool all over my toys! For the sake of all the arms and legs of my action figures, and the safety of the universe,

I have to stop her!"

Eugene jumped onto his bed. He stuck out his chest and thrust his fist into the sky, just like he had seen Super Dude do on the cover of Super Dude No. 7 when he fought the Society of Evil Babysitters.

"Queen Stinkypants must never, ever, ever, nope, never enter my secret base! So vows Captain Awesome! Heroes don't let villains

do that . . . especially stinky super-villains because you'll never get the smell out of your carpet!"

She would not, COULD NOT be allowed to enter the room. Captain Awesome doesn't like bad guys, and he also doesn't like cleaning his room.

Eugene raced to his closet and grabbed his Captain Awesome suit. Quickly, he tried to pull it on over his tennis shoes. That didn't work! He lost his balance.

"ACK!" he yelled as he fell to the floor.

"Hey! There you are!" Eugene's cape was under the bed! Standing up, he flipped the cape over his head . . . and couldn't see a thing. The cape covered his face!

He bumped into his bed and fell to the floor, again.

BONK!

That was either the sound of his head hitting the floor or THE SOUND OF QUEEN STINKY-PANTS at his door! Eugene fixed his cape as the door flung open. A blast of evil, stinky, smelly baby came at him.

"Ugh." Eugene made that face you make when you see brussels sprouts. YUCKY!

Queen Stinkypants babbled in her secret, evil baby language.

Eugene knew what every sound meant though. After she stunk up his room, she was going to drool on everything he held most dear. He had to protect his army of action figures and his collection of Super Dude comic books.

GROSS!

"No drooling on my watch, villain!" Eugene called out. Captain Awesome, and his cape, leaped into action!

CHAPTER 3

Evil Wears Pink Ribbons in Its Hair!

By Eugene

Riiiiing!

"Arrgh!" Eugene cried out.

The school bell! Was it the first bell or the second bell at Sunnyview Elementary School? Was he on time or later than late? Being late was bad, but being later than late, and on the first day at a new school, was the worst. Like green-bean-ice-cream-covered-in-broccoli-mush-sauce worse.

And just as YUCKY! Eugene cracked open the door to the school hallway. Hallways were a danger zone where the principal or vice principal patrolled— a duo of doom that would like to lock up a late student in their DUNGEON OF DETENTION. Together they would wait like furry little spiders hungry for a buzzing late fly with a backpack.

STOMP! STOMP-STOMP!

Footsteps echoed
down the empty hall!
Only a principal would
wear shoes that
STOMPED so . . .

loud . . . or someone wearing bricks on their feet. *Oh no! What if the principal's shoes are made of bricks?* Eugene gasped. *What kind of school is this place?*

Eugene dove into the nearest classroom to avoid Principal Brick Foot. He ducked as the principal lumbered by. *STOMP! STOMP-STOMP!* echoed down the hall.

"You'll never catch me, Principal Brick Foot." Eugene chuckled.

"Can I help you?" a voice behind him asked.

Eugene spun from the door and

faced ... a **TEACHER.**

"N-no," he stammered. "I was just hiding from Principal Brick Foot." The class laughed. Eugene's fingers dug into his backpack, clutching it tighter to his chest.

"I'll bet you're Eugene McGillicudy," Ms. Beasley, the teacher, said.

Eugene gasped. *How could she know that?* And then he realized the worstest, awfulest truth: *She can read minds!* Eugene grabbed his head to

stop her from sucking more thoughts from his brain.

Ms. Beasley held up her right hand and the class stopped giggling. "Eugene, I have your name on my roll sheet as the new student. Why don't you tell us *all* about yourself?"

Eugene looked around, hoping there was another new boy named Eugene standing behind him. *I'll bet Super Dude never has*

to stand in front of class and talk about himself, Eugene thought. I also bet Super Dude doesn't have a brain-sucker for a teacher.

"Ha-ha-ha!" Meredith Mooney laughed. "The new kid is a scaredy-

pants. Oh, please tell us about your oh-so-special self, Eugene. Won't you, please? My ears can't wait!"

"Meredith. Please be polite," Ms. Beasley said.

Eugene guessed that Meredith's mother must've tied the pink ribbons in her hair too tight. That would explain a lot about how she was acting.

"We are all waiting, Eugene," Ms. Beasley reminded.

Then Eugene realized something more awful than a babysitter with bad breath! The teacher and

Meredith were working together.

Like Super Dude always said:

"OHHH NO!"

Ms. Beasley had to be **MISS BEASTLY**, yet another villain destined to do really bad stuff to the mighty Captain Awesome . . . and the universe. *Like give me really hard homework*, Eugene realized. *Every night . . . just for fun!*

Not today, villain! Eugene was on to her secret plan. Ms. Beastly wanted him to tell everyone about himself so he'd reveal his secret identity as Captain Awesome! She

was using her evil sidekick, **Little Miss Stinky Pinky,** to tease him into doing it!

Looks like it was time to send evil to bed without its dessert. Miss Beastly and Little Miss Stinky Pinky would be no match for the awesomest power of **Captain Awesome!**

MI-TeE!

CHAPTER 4

Introducing Turbo

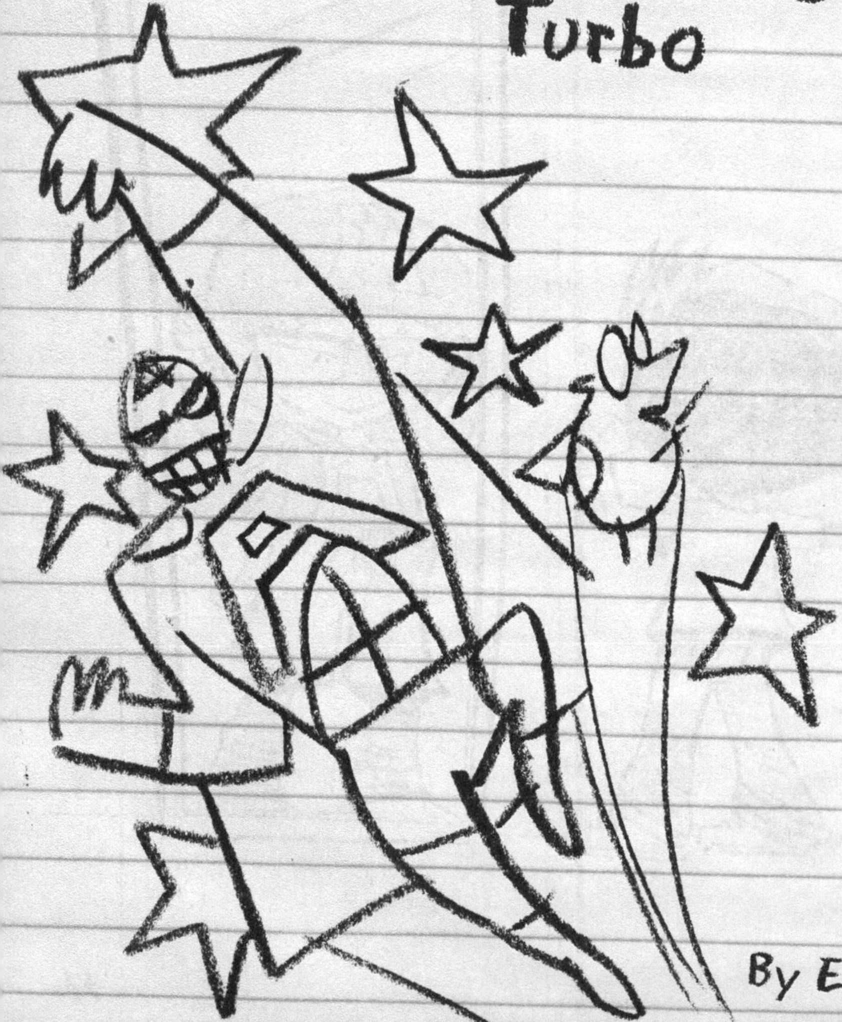

By Eugene

Eugene's second day at school was much like his first: a ringing bell and a narrow escape from Principal Brick Foot. Meredith Mooney called him Pizza Breath. So what if Eugene liked to sneak leftover pizza from the fridge for breakfast? Ms. Beasley once again called on him to stand in front of the class.

That's when

things got weirder than a frog with three eyes and a purple cowboy hat.

"How would you like to be in charge of Turbo?" Ms. Beasley asked.

What was this Operation Turbo? Some kind of supervillain trap? Was Eugene being called on to save the school? To turn up the air conditioning? To find out what was being served for lunch today? That was easy. Something GROSS!

"Turbo?" Eugene said. "What's a turbo?"

"Turbo is our class pet. He's a hamster." Ms. Beasley pointed to a cage in the back of the room. A little brown-and-white hamster was happily spinning on his squeaky metal exercise wheel.

Eugene paused. *Definitely* a trap.

"He? What?! Turbo?! I'm supposed to take care of Turbo!" Meredith whined, clearly unhappy with Ms. Beasley's choice.

"My! Me! Mine! Mere-DITH!"

"I'll do it!" Eugene blurted. Even if it was a trap, if it made Meredith unhappy, Eugene was ready to go! Eugene's heart soared like Super Dude's after that time he put Commander Barf Face in space jail in issue No. 34.

Meredith, like many villains, had a calendar to prove it was her turn to care for the little furry creature.

Unfortunately, she held it too close to Turbo's cage. The roly-poly hamster grabbed her calendar in his paws and started chomping so fast that Eugene understood why he was called "Turbo."

Turbo stopped chewing and looked up at Eugene. *Did the hamster just smile?*

"I really like this hamster," Eugene said. He was also starting to think that maybe, just maybe, Ms. Beasley wasn't so bad after all.

There was one thing about Sunnyview that was the same as Eugene's old school. He could smell the Mystery Meatloaf Surprise long before he saw it.

Eugene got his lunch and went to find a seat.

There was a sinking feeling in his stomach, and it wasn't from the smell of the Mystery Meatloaf Surprise.

It was that

horrible feeling that all new kids
get . . . where to sit in the cafeteria.
Meredith and her friends sat at one
table. No chance Eugene would sit
with them. There was an open seat
next to Mike Flinch, but he smelled
like Eugene's grandpa who spent

most of his time in his backyard digging for lost pirate treasure.

"Hey, Eugene! Yo! Over here!" Charlie Thomas Jones called out. Charlie was the one boy who *didn't* laugh when Meredith Mooney was teasing Eugene.

Eugene put down his tray and sat. Charlie brought his own lunch. He had two cans of squirt cheese and a stack of crackers. He squirted little cheese mountains on top of each cracker.

"You sure do like cheese,"

Eugene commented.

"It's better than that stuff." Charlie pointed at the rectangle on Eugene's tray. "You're eating the Mystery Meatloaf Surprise."

If a supervillain ever created a blob of gooey garbage to rob Eugene of his Captain Awesome powers, it would probably look a lot like the grayish-brown meat-thing sitting on Eugene's tray. "What's the surprise?" Eugene asked.

"You'll find out," Charlie said. "You must have an iron stomach stronger than Super Dude to eat that stuff."

"Super Dude?" Eugene was shocked. "You know who Super Dude is?"

"I have every one of his comic books!" Charlie proudly said. "I've also got a Super Dude action figure on my dresser and this talking Super Dude watch." Charlie pressed a button on his watch.

"Danger is my middle name!" the watch announced.

"Super Dude's my most favorite superhero EVER!" Eugene liked Charlie, but he wasn't sure if it was a good idea to tell him about his secret identity as Captain Awesome just yet.

Eugene took a bite of his meatloaf and made a *yuck* face.

"Surprise!" Charlie laughed.

Eugene laughed, then gagged. He spit out his bite of Mystery Meatloaf Surprise and hid it under a pile of corn. At least, he *thought* it was corn. . . .

CHAPTER 6

The Lost Hamster Weekend

Ms. Beasley had given Eugene a job, and he was going to do it right. That weekend he took Turbo home and introduced him to Mom, Dad, and Molly.

Eugene kept the cage in his bedroom, and whenever he left, he loaded Turbo into his round, plastic hamster ball—the Turbomobile—so that Turbo could follow him. Turbo joined him at the swing set, by the bathtub, and even at the dinner table.

"At least *he* keeps his cute little elbows off the table," Eugene's mom said, pointing to Turbo.

Eugene even shared his secret with his new friend.

"Turbo," Eugene whispered. "I know I can trust you with a secret, mostly because no one understands Hamster, but I want you to feel safe here because underneath these matching clothes, I'm really . . . **CAPTAIN AWESOME!**"

Turbo unleashed a tiny squeak, and Eugene smiled. A hamster's squeak was as good as a handshake, and he knew his secret would be safe.

But Sunday morning brought trouble.

Eugene slept late, sleeping sounder than Super Dude's sidekick Sergeant Super Bear during his winter hibernation in deep space.

When Eugene finally woke up, he reached over to Turbo's cage on the nightstand.

"Good morning, Turbo!" Eugene said happily. "Let's see what Mom made for breakfast! Will it be Pancakes of Power or Titanium French Toast?"

But Turbo didn't squeak an answer! He was gone!

"Turbo!" Eugene yelled. "Where are you?" Eugene jumped to his feet and pounded his fist into his palm. "This has to be the wicked work of the most super of duper supervillains . . . ever! Which one could it be?"

Eugene thought for a moment. *Superheroes have a lot of enemies, but who hamsternapped his friend Turbo?*

And more importantly, how could Eugene face Ms. Beasley and the rest of his class if they knew that Turbo was missing?

"Blah blah blah! Toldja so-toldja so-toldja so! Yackity yack yack!" He could already hear Meredith's teasing.

For the sake of Turbo—and the fear of Meredith's "nyah nyah nyah nyah nyah"s—he had to find Turbo before it was too late.

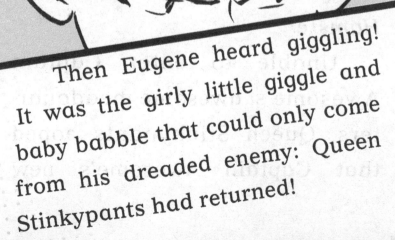

Then Eugene heard giggling! It was the girly little giggle and baby babble that could only come from his dreaded enemy: Queen Stinkypants had returned!

The giggling came from behind the door at the end of the hall. Eugene wondered what Queen Stinkypants was up to. And then it hit him!

Queen Stinkypants can speak Hamster!

Unable to enter Captain Awesome's awesome headquarters, Queen Stinkypants hoped that Captain Awesome's new friend, Turbo, would reveal all of Captain Awesome's awesome secrets.

Eugene raced back to his room to get his Captain Awesome outfit. Super Dude would never leave his outfit in a pile on the floor of *his* bedroom! That's because

superheroes are supposed to keep their bedrooms clean—especially if they still live with their parents.

Eugene ran quickly into his closet and changed into his Captain Awesome outfit.

"MI-TEE!" He shouted and ran smack into the door, bounced off, crashed into the bed, and fell to the floor.

Oops! I forgot about the door!

Captain Awesome opened the door, ran down the hallway, and grabbed the doorknob to Queen Stinkypants's Cosmic Stink Ship.

He could smell the familiar stinky stink of stinky stuff.

"Isn't it ever bathtime for supervillains?" Captain Awesome wondered. He pinched his nose and threw open the door.

"Get your diapery hands off that hamster!" Captain Awesome warned.

"Gaaah! Bwaaaah maaa moo beeemooo!" Queen Stinkypants answered.

And then Captain Awesome saw the most horrible thing possible except for the time Jill

Finbender tried to kiss him in first grade.

Turbo sat at a tiny table with Queen Stinkypants. He wore a mind-control baby bonnet and was about to be served a cup of tea!

"AAAAAAAAH! Don't drink that tea, Turbo!" Captain Awesome shouted. "It's got extra sugar in it so you can't taste the evil!"

CHAPTER 7

1 Boy-1 Hamster =
Bad News

by Eugene

Eugene was tired of thinking about how many apples he'd have if he started with four then added twelve and divided everything by four. Who wants that many apples?

Superheroes don't need math, Eugene thought. *That's why they punch things! Superheroes need to be outside so they can swing and climb on stuff.*

The bell rang. Everyone ran for the door like they were chasing after free chocolate. Eugene waited for the classroom to empty, then headed over to Turbo's cage.

"Today's a very special day," Eugene whispered. "I want you to be Captain Awesome's official sidekick. We'll call you Turbo: The Heroic Hamster, and you can use your Super Gnawing Power to—"

Panic filled Eugene's heart and backed up into his throat. Turbo was gone!

"Arrrrgh!" Eugene yelled. "Not again!"

Who could've done such a thing? Did Queen Stinkypants follow him to school?! Impossible! Her feet don't even reach the pedals on her Terror Tricycle. And he couldn't smell any of her stinky stinkiness in the air. This had to be the work of some new supermenace.

Eugene spotted a trail of cage shavings leading to the back of the room. *Good boy, Turbo!*, Eugene thought. *Leaving a trail so I can find you! What a smart little sidekick!*

The shavings led to the cubbies where the class kept their backpacks. The trail stopped at a pink backpack.

"There you are!" Ms. Beasley called out. "We're all outside for recess, Eugene."

"But-I-It's-Just-Um-Ah!" Eugene stammered.

"Go get some fresh air, sunshine, and monkey bars, kiddo."

Eugene sighed and trudged into the hall. Super Dude would never leave a man behind enemy lines. Sure, Turbo was a hamster, but Super Dude would never leave a hamster behind either. Even to go play on monkey bars.

Neither would Eugene.

"Hold on, little guy," Eugene whispered, even though Turbo couldn't hear him. "I'll be back for you.

I PROMISE. . . ."

Kids screamed. They kicked balls, played games, and ran around like pretend airplanes in an imaginary sky.

Except for Eugene. He sat cross-legged near the tetherball courts. He had failed in his first mission for Ms. Beasley. Who would ever trust him with a small caged animal again? Not even the cafeteria's Mystery Meatloaf Surprise made him feel this sick. Then Meredith Mooney stuck her tongue out at him. He didn't feel like much of a hero now.

"Hey, there, Eugenio! Eugene!" Eugene was so lost in thought that he barely heard Charlie. "You look like your sister spilled gravy on your favorite issue of Super Dude."

"Worse, Charlie. Much worse. Turbo's been hamsternapped."

"No!" Charlie gasped.

"And I think Little Miss

Stinky—I mean Meredith did it."

"NO!" Charlie gasped even louder.

Eugene stopped talking so Charlie could catch his breath.

"We can't let her get away with it!" Charlie exclaimed. "The Fans of Super Dude Society won't stand for it!"

"The Fans of Super Dude Society?"

"I thought we needed a name for our club," Charlie said.

"We have a club?" Eugene asked.

"Sure! It's the 'Fans of Super Dude Society'! We friends gotta stick together."

Eugene smiled. Not because he was in a club called, awesomely enough, the Fans of Super Dude Society, or FsssDsss for short, but because Charlie had referred to him as a friend! MI-TEE!

Eugene stood up, suddenly filled with awesomeness once more . . . and was smacked in the head by the tetherball.

"OW!"

"Sorry!" Ryan Fitzpatrick said.

Eugene had a plan. Never sit next to the tetherball court again. Okay, Eugene had *two* plans, and the other was as cool as a Super Dude plan. "But I'm going to need *your* help after recess!" he said to Charlie.

"Anything for a fellow member of the FsssDsss!" Charlie replied.

CHAPTER 9

Captain Awesome Saves the Day and the Hamster

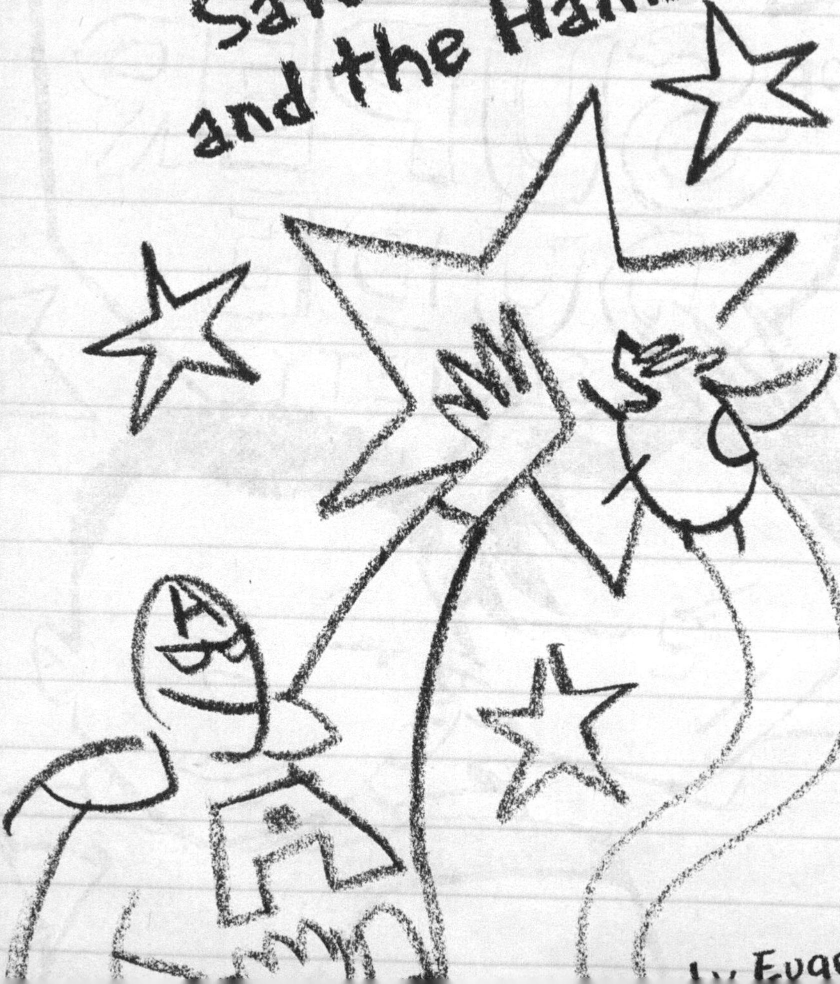

Ms. **Beasley started class** with geography. "Can anyone tell me the capital of France?" she asked.

That's when Eugene gave Charlie the thumbs-up.

"Help!"

"No, Charlie," she corrected. "It's Paris."

"No! No! No! Help!" Charlie repeated. "My desk's gone crazy!"

Charlie's desk rocked like a wild bull. His feet bounced the desk into Bernie Melnick's, which fell into Marlo Craven's and then into Evan Mason's.

"Charlie Thomas Jones!"

"I just can't . . . stop . . . it, Ms. Beasley!" Charlie gasped. "This is the . . . strongest, most . . .

powerful desk . . . I've ever . . . seen!"

While Charlie distracted the class, Eugene ran to his cubby and unzipped the secret compartment of his backpack. He took out his Captain Awesome suit, straightened on his cape, and got ready to save his hamster friend.

"Time to get MI-TEE!"

Eugene raced to the front of the class, his towel-cape fluttering behind him. He skidded to a stop before Ms. Beasley, who met him with a raised brow.

"Hold, citizen! For I, Captain Awesome, have something to say!"

Charlie's mouth dropped open. His desk stopped moving. The class sat in silence and waited for the caped hero of goodness's next words.

Captain Awesome spun and pointed a finger toward Turbo's cage. "Earlier today I found out that your class pet—the hamster known as Turbo—had disappeared!"

The class gasped in shock, and so did Ms. Beasley.

"Someone took our Turbo?" Ms. Beasley asked, a little surprised she was talking to a boy dressed in a superhero getup in the middle of her classroom.

Captain Awesome pointed to the trail of shavings that led from the cage to the backpack cubbies. "Gaze upon the trail of shavings! It goes right to the backpack with a pink ribbon! And we *all* know who wears a *pink* ribbon!"

"My Uncle Lewis!" Mike Flinch called out.

"No!" Captain Awesome continued. **"Meredith Mooney!"**

The students gasped again. Even Ms. Beasley was speechless for a moment. Meredith put her hands on her head, trying to hide the ribbons.

"Those are some serious accusations, Captain . . .

what was it again?" Ms. Beasley asked.

"Awesome, ma'am. Captain Awesome. As in 'Wow! He's AWESOME!'"

"You have no proof it was me, Captain

Grossface!" Meredith defended. "I'm not the only one who wears pink ribbons. How do you know it wasn't Mike's uncle Lewis?"

"Because I don't think Mike's uncle Lewis has a pink backpack!"

Captain Awesome looked quickly to Mike to make sure. Mike shook his head no.

Captain Awesome picked up the pink backpack at the end of the shavings trail. He read the name tag. "This pink backpack with the pink ribbon has a name tag that reads: 'Meredith Mooney.' Let's see what's inside."

Meredith jumped from her desk. "You can't do that! That's *my* backpack! Ms. Beasley!"

"My. Me. Mine. Mere-DITH," Captain

Awesome said and unzipped the backpack.

Turbo raced out and climbed onto Captain Awesome. "Just like Super Dude says: 'Danger is my middle name,'" Captain Awesome whispered to his furry sidekick.

Ms. Beasley turned to Meredith. "Well . . . ?"

"It's all true!" Meredith sniffed. "I took Turbo and hid him in my backpack. I wanted to be the one to take care of him, not Eugene. It was my turn, not his."

"Meredith . . ." Ms. Beasley began calmly. "I didn't ask Eugene to watch Turbo to punish you. I just wanted to make Eugene feel welcome. It's not easy being someplace new, and sometimes it helps to know that there are people who care."

Captain Awesome tried to hide his smile. It looked like Ms. Beasley wasn't a brain-sucker after all.

Captain Awesome took Turbo in his hands and carried him back to his cage. "And now I, Captain Awesome, must leave, for there are other children with other missing class pets and stuff like that. Good-bye, children of Ms. Beasley's class. I'll be seeing you! Don't forget to brush your teeth!"

Captain Awesome raced out the door. Then a second later he raced back in.

"And feel free to give that kid Eugene all your desserts at lunch time!"

And just like that, Captain Awesome was gone.

Minutes later, Eugene came back into the classroom.

"So did I miss anything?" he
asked with a smile.

"This was a pretty—*cough,*
cough—awesome day," Charlie said
as he and Eugene walked home
after school. "Not everybody gets
to rescue a hamster from the bad
guys."

"If comic books teach us anything," Eugene said, "it's
that Badness always
loses to Goodness."

Eugene was put
in charge of Turbo,

SUPER DUDE

THE SUPEREST DUDE OF ALL!

#902

S

REMEMBER, KIDS—
BADNESS ALWAYS LOSES!!

and Meredith lost recess for a week.

"Dude, you have no idea how cool it is that you're a superhero!" Charlie said, then carefully looked around. "Can I tell you a secret? I'm a superhero, too!"

Eugene was shocked. "No!"

"Yes!" Charlie said. "I'm the one and only Nacho Cheese Man! I have the power of canned cheese." Charlie pulled out a plastic bottle of canned cheese from his backpack. He popped the cap and blasted the letter C against a tree trunk.

"I knew you liked cheese,"

Eugene said. "But who knew it would give you superpowers!"

"I've been practicing," Charlie said. "You never know when you might need some cheese to

fight the forces of evil." Charlie held up a second can. "This one's taco-flavored to put a rumble in evil's tummy!"

"This is great news, Charlie! Two superheroes to fight Sunnyview's bad guys are way better than one!" Eugene said.

"Yeah! Let's form a superhero club," Charlie suggested.

"We'll need a name." Eugene thought for a moment. "Like the

SUNNYVIEW SUPERHERO SQUAD."

"I like it!" Charlie said.

"Together we shall defeat the forces of evil!" Eugene stood with his hand on his hips. "We'll find missing library books! Solve the riddles of the school's heating system! Figure out what Sudoku means!"

"Yeah! Now we need a slogan! And a theme song!"

"One thing at a time, Nacho Cheese Man, one thing at a time."

Together with Turbo, the boys headed home. Another day was ending.

Another day had been saved.

And Meredith? She was still stuck at school, cleaning out Turbo's cage.

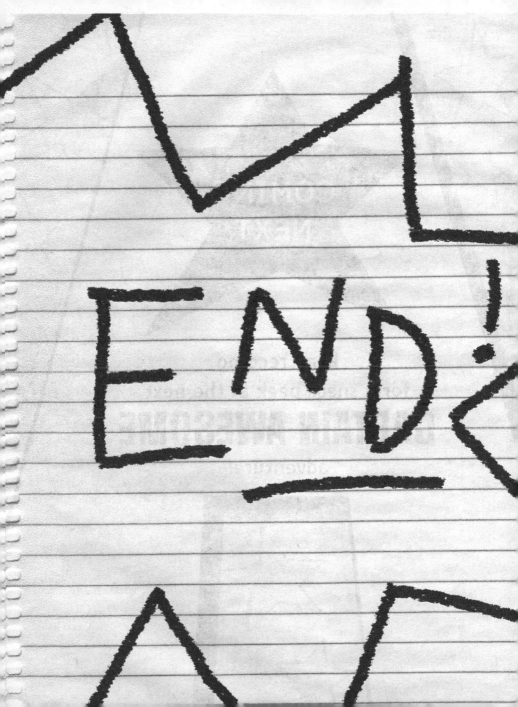

THE END!

CAPTAIN AWESOME VS. NACHO CHEESE MAN

"By the super MI-TEE force of Captain Awesome and the canned cheese power of Nacho Cheese Man, I call this Sunnyview Superhero Squad tree house sleepover meeting to order."

THUMP!

Eugene McGillicudy banged a wooden spoon against an empty shoebox. The Sunnyview Superhero Squad meeting had begun.

Sunnyview? Superhero? Squad? That's right! Eugene and his best friend, Charlie Thomas Jones, were not just ordinary students at

Sunnyview Elementary, they also had super secret superhero identities. Eugene was Captain Awesome and Charlie was Nacho Cheese Man. Together, along with Captain Awesome's hamster sidekick (and the class pet), Turbo, they formed the Sunnyview Superhero Squad to protect the universe from bad guys.

"Hurry up," Charlie said. "The brownies are waiting!"

Brownies! Yum! The perfect superhero snack! thought Eugene. Evil doesn't stand a chance against chocolate fudge.

With the latest issue of Super Dude completed, Eugene rubbed Turbo's furry head. "Good night, buddy."

"Good night, Turbo," Charlie said and clicked off his flashlight.

Soon both heroes were fast asleep and the tree house was filled with the squeak of Turbo's exercise wheel as it spun round and round.

Then there was a *BUMP!* Eugene opened one sleepy eye.

That's probably nothing.

Then he heard it again. *THUMP!* His other eye snapped open.

That's something. My Captain Awesome Danger Sense is tingling!

Something was in the yard. Eugene sat up in his sleeping bag and listened. *RATTLE!*

Could it be?!

"Grrrrr! Rowl! SNARL!"

Yes, it was! His furry, old enemy Mr. Drools had returned! Mr. Drools, the hairy four-legged monster from the Howling Paw Nebula, whose drooly jaws loved to chomp everything Eugene held most dear.

And worse, his evil Drool House was right next door to Eugene's home. Mr. Drools had turned the once normal house into his own "barkyard."

He's stolen three Frisbees, popped a soccer ball, eaten the cover off a baseball, and ripped up my kite like an old sock! *What's he after this time?!* Eugene wondered. Then he realized something awful. . . . NOOOOOOOOO! NOT MY SUPER DUDE ISSUE No. 429!?

Eugene jumped up without unzipping his sleeping bag. He hopped like the rare hopping caterpillars of Mothonia in Super Dude

No. 97. He hopped on his flashlight, lost his balance, and fell to the wooden floor.

Eugene crawled from his sleeping bag.

Splinter!

"Ouch! Ouch! Ouch!"

Since superheroes can do anything, Eugene quickly pulled out the splinter. He felt around for his flashlight and clicked it on.

This was a nighttime job for Captain Awesome and Nacho Cheese Man!

"Wake up!" he whispered to

Charlie. "Mr. Drools is in his bark-yard next door!"

Charlie shot out of his sleeping bag like he'd been stuck with a pin. He grabbed the emergency can of nacho cheese he kept under his pillow.

Eugene placed Turbo into the Turbomobile. They would need the power of two heroes and one side-kick to stop the barking, slobbery madness of Mr. Drools.

"Go chase your tail, Mr. Drools! You'll never get my comic book!" Captain Awesome called down from the tree house. "Your slobber is useless on this night!"

"I must warn you now . . ." Nacho Cheese Man called out, "I've got cheese!"

The trio of heroes climbed down from their tree house moon base and onto the cold surface of the moon. . . .

No. 1

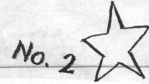

No. 2

No. 3